at all, Lynn Frazer."

He stepped forward and lifted her chin with his fingertips until he was gazing directly into her eyes. "One moment you're haranguing me, delving for the secrets of my past. The next you're erecting a wall to keep me out."

"I was doing just fine until you came along," she whispered, staring up at him.

"And now I'm invading your house, encroaching on your territory and making you uncomfortable." He dropped his hand but maintained contact with her eyes a moment longer. "Who are you afraid of? Me—or yourself?"

Without waiting for her response, he strode from the house, banging the door behind him. He glanced back. What was it about her? Why was he baiting her like that? He didn't need the entanglement any more than she did.

Barbara Stewart says that one of her first memories is of being taken to the library by her father and bringing home stacks of books as tall as she was. She's been reading—and writing—ever since. But she didn't begin writing professionally until she'd been teaching it for ten years, when she decided that actually *doing* it had to be easier! Her decision to concentrate on romance was a natural one—she says she loves happy endings.

This book is dedicated
to the memory of
Daryl Stewart Robinson.

LOVE ME NOT

Barbara Stewart

W⦿RLDWIDE ®

TORONTO • NEW YORK • LONDON
AMSTERDAM • PARIS • SYDNEY • HAMBURG
STOCKHOLM • ATHENS • TOKYO • MILAN
MADRID • WARSAW • BUDAPEST • AUCKLAND

Special thanks and acknowledgment to
Barbara Rae Robinson

ISBN 0-373-83276-1

LOVE ME NOT

Copyright © 1994 Harlequin Enterprises B. V.

One

"Lynn Frazer!"

She ignored the intrusive voice coming from somewhere behind her and tightened her grip on the wooden railing of the weathered pier as she stared at the shrouded horizon in the distance. *Oh, Nick, where are you?* she silently repeated.

"Hey! What are you trying to do, kill yourself?"

The crashing waves rolling toward shore muffled the deep voice in the distance. A stiff breeze pelted her with raindrops from the dark dense clouds overhead and whipped strands of hair into her face. She brushed at the strands, her eyes focusing on the roiling sea and a solitary mast in the distance. Someone was still out there among the tossing waves. Trying to catch a few more fish. Just like Nick had been doing that day when his boat was caught in a sudden spring squall.

Footsteps echoed on the planks behind her.

Lynn heaved a sigh. Those who knew her left her alone when she was on the pier. They understood.

As she reluctantly turned, a strong hand grabbed her arm and yanked her several feet away from the railing. "You'll get washed out to sea!" A stranger's voice boomed.

A breaking wave surged over the end of the pier, soaking her shoes and the bottom of her jeans. She shivered, as much from resentment at having her solitary vigil interrupted as from the cold water.

"I'm all right," she said, brushing off the grasp. "Don't get so excited. This is only a mild October storm." She pulled her jacket more tightly around her.

Then she shifted her gaze to the man towering over her. And stared.

Rugged, powerful, masculine. Those were the words that came to her. She stepped back. In the waning light of dusk, his eyes were dark and penetrating, almost as if he could see right into her soul.

She trembled, her apprehension growing. "How... how'd you know my name and where to find me?"

"Pete Duncan told me."

At the mention of Pete's name, she exhaled the breath she realized she was holding. Pete was too good a friend to send someone to her he didn't trust.

The stranger reached for her again. "Let's get off this rickety pier," he said. "I need to talk to you." His voice was gruff and hard.

"What about?" She sidestepped, avoiding his grasp. The water in her shoes chilled her feet. A hot bath would feel good right now.

"Let's talk about it on shore." He strode away from her, obviously expecting her to follow.

"This pier can take a stronger storm than this," she muttered as another wave broke over the weathered boards and swept toward her. Conceding defeat, she reluctantly headed for shore.

The man was waiting for her at the street end of the pier.

"Who are you and why did Pete tell you where to find me?" she asked, studying the rugged contours of his face in the pale glow from the lone streetlight.

"The name's Vince Coulter."

"So you're that friend of his from Long Island—the one who was supposed to be here a week ago."

"Yeah. Had a bit of car trouble along the way—actually a lot of car trouble." He laughed, a deep rumble with no joy in it.

They crossed the narrow street and stepped up on the boardwalk in front of the only grocery store in Garrett Cove.

"What do you want from me?" she asked.

"I need to sell some pottery I brought along. I used practically all the money I had just to get here. I need some cash."

"Didn't Pete tell you I only take pottery on consignment?" The words came out more petulant-sounding than she'd intended.

He frowned. "Will you look at what I have before you make that kind of decision?"

She faced him, unsure where her peevishness was coming from. Maybe it was her wet feet. Or being interrupted out on the pier. She tried to make her tone matter-of-fact. "I've only bought three pieces out right in the past year. They were unique. None of the other potters who sell through my shop have made anything like them."

. "Mine are unique."

"I've heard that before." She started down the wooden boardwalk fronting the row of businesses that made up the commercial district of the tiny town on the central California coast.

"Well, let me at least show you what I have."

She stopped under the awning of the store and turned back to him. "I'd like to change my wet clothes. Can't it wait until tomorrow?"

"I don't believe in wasting time," he replied. " have lots to do tomorrow if I'm going to get settled in here."

The encroaching darkness shadowed his features making him appear almost sinister. But Pete *had* talked of Vince Coulter in glowing terms. He said they'd grown up in the same New York neighborhood and had remained friends, despite the distance that had separated them the past few years.

"All right," she said reluctantly. "Get your work and meet me at my shop." She pointed to the next building. "The one in the middle. I'll be back in a few minutes."

She left him standing and walked around the end of the building and up a slight incline toward her house on the top of the closest knoll.

Ten minutes later she returned to the boardwalk in dry shoes and jeans, curious to see what Vince Coulter had with him. Pete only sent artists to her whose work met her standards.

Vince was standing by the door to her shop, a cardboard box cradled in his arms. She unlocked the door and flipped on the interior lights. "Come on in," she said, staring into dark eyes as cold as the sea and wondering what had happened to the man to make him so harsh and bitter. Then she remembered Pete had mentioned an accident.

"Thanks," Vince replied. "I appreciate your taking the time to look at what I have."

Something in that low somber voice told her he was sincere. A slight spark of interest kindled inside her. She tried to ignore the feeling and walked to the counter in the middle of the room.

Display cases and shelves lined the walls of the shop and were filled with all manner of pottery, glassware and other gift items. The scent of candles and potpourri mingled and permeated the entire room.

Vince followed her into the store and set the box on the counter next to the cash register. She sidled around to the rear of the counter, letting the wooden structure serve as a barrier between them. Something about this man unsettled her.

Because her curiosity had gotten the better of her, she took another good look at him, trying not to be too obvious. Faded jeans hugged narrow hips, and a flannel shirt and jacket encased broad shoulders. He was too rough around the edges to be called handsome. Compelling—yes, that was a better word to describe him. Then she added the word "brazen" to her assessment as she realized he was boldly looking her over in return. "Let's see what you have," she said in her best professional tone, while wondering if this was a man she wanted to do business with at all.

"Here's the first box. I have three more of the same kind of stuff in my van," he said as he opened the lid and carefully, almost reverently, unwrapped the packing material from around a teapot and six matching cups and set the pieces carefully on the counter. Then he brought out a delicate bowl in the same intricate pale blue pattern, handling it with the same meticulous care.

Lynn recognized the superb artistry of the work even before she picked up the bowl to examine it more closely. A strange excitement grew inside her as she slowly turned the piece of pottery in her hand, inspecting the exquisite hand-painted detail—a blue-petal design interwoven with seemingly fragile greenery. She smiled. Vince was right. His work was unique.

"Can't you give me something for these?" he asked, stepping back.

She set the bowl on the counter and turned her smile to the man towering over her. "You have a rare talent, Vince. I'll have to make an exception for you." Mentally she calculated the value of the pieces in front of her and multiplied by four. "Only one problem," she said, her brow wrinkling in a frown. "I'm not sure

I can afford to buy all you have right now if the other three boxes are filled with things as good as these.''

Distress flared briefly in his eyes before they resumed their cold dark stare. "You're the only show in town," he said. "I'm at your mercy."

She ran a finger over the intricate pattern on the delicate teapot, impressed with the smoothness of the surface. "I can give you part of the money to start with," she said, and named a figure. "I'm sure these will sell." Her eyes met his. "You have to understand. This is a slow time of year for beach crowds and the businesses that cater to them."

He started replacing the pieces in the box. "I need to find a place to live, a place where I can set up a studio."

"As I get more cash from sales, I can give you more. That's the best I can do right now."

"Then I'll have to take it. I'll go get the other three boxes."

"Just a minute," she said, and went to her tiny office in back of the shop, closing the door behind her. She extracted her checkbook from the floor safe and wrote out a check. Returning to the outer shop, she handed it to him. "You can bring the other three boxes tomorrow. I trust you," she said, looking up at him as she realized she did.

"Thanks," he said, stuffing the check into his pocket without looking at it.

When the door of the shop had closed behind them, she turned to him. "Well, good night, Vince."

"Uh...I'll walk you up to your house. Awfully dark now, what with the clouds and rain."

"That isn't necessary." A certain wariness crept into her voice.

"But I want to." His voice was quiet, the harshness gone.

She shrugged. "Suit yourself," she said, and stepped off the boardwalk onto the muddy path leading up the hill to her driveway. The light rain continued to fall.

Halfway up the driveway he stopped. "That your garage?" he asked, looking at the wooden structure not ten feet from the house. The raised overhead door revealed her little blue Honda off to one side.

"Yes," she said hesitantly, her brow furrowing. "Why?"

"Pete said you had a nice big garage," he replied, "with a good, solid concrete slab for a floor. May I take a look?" At her nod he strode to the weather-beaten wooden structure and stopped at the door. She followed closely behind.

"What's so interesting about a garage?" she asked. She flicked on the light switch by the door.

He kicked at the concrete floor. "I know Pete was joking when he said it, but he told me you had a garage big and sturdy enough for a studio." He turned to her. "I need a place to set up a temporary studio. I'd like to rent your garage—until I have enough money to get the kind of place I need."

"Sorry, it's not for rent." The words came out in a rush, automatically. She couldn't even consider such a request.

He ignored her and stepped into the middle of the garage. She put her hands on her hips and watched him as he spun around, taking in all the details of piled furniture, boxes, dirt and grime. His shoulders straightened and he seemed infused with a new energy. When he turned back to her, his mouth had curved into a genuine grin and his dark forbidding eyes now blazed with a sudden fervor. He took several steps toward her.

"Please think about it," he said. "I have to have a place to work."

"You aren't listening to me. I said it's not for rent," she repeated, turning away to hide her rising panic. She didn't want anyone so close, especially not a man like Vince Coulter. If Nick truly *was* dead, she intended to build herself a life so independent she'd never need anyone else again. That way she'd never be hurt again.

He spun around once more, his eyes glowing with an inner fire. "I can almost feel the wet clay in my hands," he said, "spinning on the wheel. . . . It's been a long time."

"No!" she said, then realized with a pang of guilt that he'd have the money to rent something if she'd been able to give him what four boxes of his pottery were really worth.

"I could get Pete to help me put in another door, so I wouldn't have to use the overhead door all the time," he said, excitement permeating his voice. "I can move the rest of this stuff to one corner. Properly stacked, it'd give me enough room to work."

She felt the warmth of Vince's hand close around her arm, and a tingle of awareness flitted through her body.

"Please, Lynn. At least consider it. I need a place to work so I can make a new start out here on the Coast. It's very important to me."

She glanced down at the strong hand on her arm. How long had it been since a man had touched her . . . made her feel like a woman? He pulled her around to face him, a wide smile on his face. A beguiling smile. He did have a certain charm when he chose to use it— too much charm to be so near.

She pulled out of his grasp. "I can't," she said, with no attempt to keep the desperation out of her voice. "I can't let you use it."

"I don't see why not. You'd benefit, too." His voice had completely lost its hard edge and had a certain buoyancy. "I'd be turning out pottery for you to sell in your shop."

He looked deep into her eyes and she felt her resistance slowly eroding. Something about this man spoke to some inner need in her, a need she didn't quite understand.

But she'd be unfaithful to Nick even to consider such an arrangement, wouldn't she? A strange man working in the garage? Another thought filtered into her consciousness. *Had* Pete been joking when he'd told Vince about her garage? Or had he really thought it was a good idea for Vince to work here? She wished Pete was here now so she could ask his advice.

"I hope your hesitation means you're reconsidering," Vince said, his eyes still holding hers.

She stalled a little longer, trying to think of other excuses. But all she could think of were reasons why she *could* do it. Added income from the rent. More lovely things to sell in the shop. Helping a friend of Pete's. Helping a talented artist in need. Besides, she'd be down at her shop most of the time and wouldn't have to see him every day....

"All right," she said, her voice almost a whisper.

Two

Vince sighed with relief. He'd been so sure she'd stick with her refusal, despite all that hesitation. "Thanks," he said. "You don't know what this means to me."

Her lips drew into a soft smile. "Let's just say I'm doing it because you're a friend of Pete's."

He cocked a brow. "Pete's going to be surprised when I tell him."

She tilted her chin and her smile widened, but he saw a certain sadness in her light blue eyes. "I owe Pete—and Maria—more than I can ever repay. They helped me through some really rough times."

Vince nodded but didn't say anything. Pete had told him about her husband's fishing boat capsizing with four of them aboard. Two survived and two hadn't. Pete felt guilty because he was one of the lucky ones.

Vince gazed at her and felt the stirrings of interest. Pete said he'd like her. And, despite their rather stormy—in more ways than one—introduction out on the pier, she seemed to be thawing toward him.

He liked her small pert mouth. And her tiny tipped-up nose. She reminded him of that petite blonde he'd met at the gallery in Manhattan last year. Lynn had a certain genuineness. A completely natural woman. Not even a hint of makeup on her face. And her long blond hair hung about her shoulders unrestrained. He liked that, too.

Only one more thing to do. He wouldn't be able to sleep tonight if he didn't tell her the truth. He thought of the tea set and bowl he'd left in the shop. And the three boxes of similar ware in his van.

"Lynn . . . there's something I haven't told you yet. Something you should know." He frowned. He didn't like admitting his weaknesses. "Those pieces I just gave you—I won't be making any more like that." His words came out in a rush. Afraid to look at her face, afraid he might see disgust there, he stared at the concrete floor.

"An auto accident—two years ago," he continued. "A deep cut on my right wrist that damaged the nerves. I can't do the intricate painting anymore, and I'm not even sure I can do the delicate shapes of the pieces."

"Oh, dear." She said the words softly.

He felt her hand on his arm and turned to her. "I'm so sorry," she said, a tear glistening in the corner of her eye.

"I don't want your pity," he snapped, and brushed her hand away. "I have to learn some new techniques for throwing pots, since my right arm no longer functions the way it used to. That's what I'll be working on in your garage. What I need is a chance, a new start."

He hadn't meant to react so fiercely. She looked stricken and afraid. From somewhere deep inside, he felt the sudden urge to gather her in his arms and reassure her. But he resisted the impulse. That was something he might have done before the accident. Now he had too much work to do. No time for a woman, especially one with problems of her own. Besides, he didn't have anything to offer a woman, any woman. He'd be lucky if he could still support himself as a potter. But he had to try.

"See you tomorrow," he said, leaving her standing in the garage.

"Lynn! I can't believe you've done this," Carol Snyder said in her usual big-sister tone. "You rented your garage to a man you don't even know?"

"He's a friend of Pete's." Lynn picked up a wool duster and swished it over the shelves and the pottery pieces.

"And any friend of Pete's is a friend of yours...." Carol shook her head, but a smile played on her lips.

Lynn smiled back at her sister, a diminutive brunette with laughing blue eyes. "Don't worry about it. Believe me, the garage is as close as the man's getting."

Carol quirked an eyebrow. "Why do you say that?"

Her tone implied more than casual interest. Lynn realized she'd revealed too much already but couldn't take back the words. "No man gets inside my house except family or Pete." She said the words in as even a tone as she could manage. She couldn't admit, especially to Carol, that Vince Coulter intrigued her.

Carol leaned against the counter in the middle of the shop. "Are you going to pine away for Nick forever? He's dead, Lynn. He won't be back."

Lynn sighed. "You don't know that he's dead any more than I do. I still can't help hoping that some foreign fishing boat picked him up and he has amnesia and is wandering around the world not knowing where he belongs...."

"And his memory will be miraculously restored and he'll come sailing back to you," Carol finished for her. "You know that's not logical. We've looked at all the possibilities, time and time again. Nick is dead." She enunciated the words carefully. "Pete saw him roll off the deck as the boat turned over."

Lynn lifted her chin stubbornly. "Tim's body was found right away. Pete and Dave were rescued by the coast guard. Someone else could have found Nick floating on some debris and carried him far away from here."

Carol threw up her hands and shook her head. "You can't really believe that."

"I want to," Lynn replied. "That way I at least have hope."

"But you have that Late Death Registration issued by the court," Carol said. "Nick is dead," she repeated. "When are you going to come to your senses and accept it?"

Lynn looked directly at her. "That death registration is just a piece of paper. It proves nothing. It means nothing. Larry should have left things as they were."

"We all thought you'd accept the court's ruling," Carol said. "That's why Larry went ahead and gathered the evidence and petitioned the court. If you'd only look at all the evidence and the transcripts, you'd realize Nick couldn't possibly be alive. Larry has said he'll bring the entire file home from the office any time you want to see it."

"Just because your husband's a lawyer doesn't mean he had to interfere," Lynn said.

"It's been a year and a half," Carol replied. "Plenty of time for you to accept that Nick's gone and not coming back. Do you really want to be alone for the rest of your life?"

"Yes," Lynn answered automatically. Then an image of the dark stranger—of Vince—crept into her consciousness. Could she ever love again? No. No, absolutely not.

Carol started for the door. "You're impossible. Just as stubborn as you've always been."

"I can take care of myself," Lynn said. "I have my business. I'm self-supporting. I don't have to depend on a man, and I never will again."

Carol stopped just short of the door. "Look, I didn't come here to argue with you." A smile softened her features. "Can you get away for a couple of hours on Sunday for Dad's birthday dinner?"

"Make it after five and there's no problem. That's when I close the shop."

"All right. Six o'clock, at our house." Carol reached for the doorknob just as the door flew open. She stepped back, wide-eyed.

Vince strode in, a box in his hands. "I have the other three boxes. Where do you want them?"

"Set them down anywhere," Lynn said. "I'll unpack them when I decide where I'm going to display all the new pieces." She smiled at the look of surprise on Carol's face and introduced the two of them. Curiosity kept Carol from leaving, for which Lynn was glad. She'd just as soon not be alone with Vince.

As for Vince, he seemed ill at ease with an audience. He brought in the other two boxes, then approached her. "Pete will be here in a couple of hours with a door he found, and we'll start working on the garage. Uh . . . could I use your keys to back your car out of the garage? I'll start cleaning while I wait for Pete."

"Sure." Lynn retrieved the keys from her purse in the office and handed them to him. He took them with a half smile and left hurriedly.

Carol grinned broadly, a look of mischief in her eyes. "On second thought, maybe you're not as crazy as you seem. See you later."

"What's that supposed to mean?" Lynn asked as Carol closed the door behind her. She let out an exasperated sigh and turned to her task, unpacking the pottery in the three boxes and making a list of the contents. Then she rearranged the items displayed on the shelves along one side of the shop to accommodate the new ones. With each piece she placed on the shelves, her excitement grew. The work was exquisite. Vince Coulter was an artist.

She sighed. What a shame to lose the ability to exercise such talent. How she wished he could still do this kind of intricate painting.

She picked up a vase. There she was—wishing again. Wishing things were different from the way they were. Just like with Nick. She was always wishing his body had been found. Then she'd know for sure in her heart that he was dead.

Cradling the delicate vase in her hands, she studied the design. Lavender blossoms—iris with green spiky leaves. Soft, ethereal lavender blossoms, looking as if they were floating on a breeze.

She set the slender vase aside. This one she'd buy for herself and put it on the little buffet against the wall in the living room. She couldn't bring herself to sell all the pieces, though she knew without a doubt she'd be able to.

At noon Lynn closed the shop, put her Be Back Soon sign in the window and headed up the hill for a quick lunch. Pete's green truck, loaded with lumber and tools, and a maroon van sat in the driveway. Her Honda had been moved around to the back. The left wall of the garage sported a gaping hole where Pete was fitting a new door, one with a window in the top of it.

The overhead garage door was up and she could see Vince pounding nails in what looked like shelves. Pete saw her first and met her in the driveway. "Lynn, I want to thank you for the way you're helping Vince. You won't be sorry."

She smiled at the sandy-haired man in front of her and realized he was at least a couple of inches shorter than Vince, then wondered why she'd even thought of it.

"I hope I won't be sorry," she said. "I don't even know the man. But he's your friend. Let's just say I'm doing this for you." She looked up and saw Vince watching her from inside the garage. She waved to him, then turned back to Pete.

Pete grinned. "Whatever your reasons, I appreciate it. And so does Vince. I've known him for years. He's a great guy."

"I believe you."

He tilted his head. "Come on now, fess up. Aren't you just a little bit interested in him?"

She glared at Pete. "Don't you even dare *think* of playing matchmaker," she said in a low but forceful tone. "I'm not interested in any man, and you of all people should know that."

He chucked her under the chin. "Someday, my sweet little friend, you'll change your tune. I just hope you don't wait too long. You're missing out on a lot in life."

She frowned. "Nick was your best friend. How can you say that?"

"Nick's gone," Pete replied. "You're still here—a living breathing woman who needs someone to love."

"I have lots of family and friends around here. That's enough for me."

"It won't always be." Pete shrugged. "I have a great-aunt who lost her husband at an early age and never remarried. She's the most crotchety old biddy I've ever known. I don't want to see you end up like her."

Lynn laughed. "Pete, you worry too much. I'm not your responsibility."

"Yes, you are," he said, his voice suddenly serious. "Whether you want to be or not."

Her brow wrinkled into a frown. "I can take care of myself. I prefer to be alone."

He looked her straight in the eye, his face solemn. "About a year before Nick died, we made a pact," he said. "He was to take care of Maria and the kids if anything ever happened to me. I agreed to look after you if something happened to him. And I know Nick wouldn't want you to be alone for the rest of your life."

"You've been a good friend, and I appreciate everything you've done for me. Just don't overstep the bounds of friendship by trying to find me another husband. I don't want one."

Vince ambled out of the garage. "My ears are burning. Everything all right?"

"No problem, old buddy," Pete said. "Just a friendly discussion," he added, with emphasis on the "friendly."

Vince seemed a bit nervous as he turned to Lynn. "One more favor to ask of you," he said. "I hope you don't mind if I park my van next to the garage. I'm

going to have to sleep in it for a while. All the places
for rent around here cost more than I have right now."

"Where'd you sleep last night?" she asked, a mild
panic returning at the thought of his being right outside.

"Pete's couch." He grinned. "And I had three little rug rats piling on me about seven this morning."

Pete laughed. "No wonder you won't stay with us."

"Oh, it's not the kids," Vince said. "They're no
problem. I just don't want to impose on you and Maria."

"You wouldn't be imposing," Pete said.

"I don't know how long it will be before I can rent
a place," Vince said. "I slept in the van all the way
across the country. A little while longer won't hurt me.
There'll be plenty of room after I get all my tools and
equipment out of it and into the garage."

"That doesn't look like a completely, uh, outfitted
van," Lynn said with a grimace.

"No problem. I'll use that rest room down on the
beach." Vince gestured toward the gray building to the
right of the pier. "And Maria's offered to let me
shower at their house. Everything's taken care of." He
grinned broadly.

Lynn simply stared at him. She'd be able to look out
her bedroom window and see the van, with him in it,
every night. Too close.

Her comfortable complacent life-style was suddenly being eroded and she seemed powerless to do
anything about it. All she wanted was for Vince Coulter to go away! But how could she back out now?

Three

"Aren't you the least bit curious to see what I've done to your garage this past week?" Vince asked. He stood in the center of the driveway, blocking Lynn's path as she headed home for the evening.

She stopped a good six feet away from him. "I've peeked in the window a time or two," she admitted. In fact, she'd tried her best to ignore the activity going on so close to her house, just as she'd tried to ignore the man himself. She let her eyes roam over his sturdy male physique and wondered what it was about him she perceived as dangerous. That's when she felt the pounding in her chest. She turned away, intending to walk around him and retreat to the safety of her house.

He reached for her arm. "Come here. Just for a minute." He gestured with a nod of his head. "It's finished—my studio." The expression on his face indicated a need for her approval.

She pulled away from his grip and took a deep breath. "All right, I'll come look—just for a minute."

He led her to the door of the garage and opened it with a flourish. She could see the pride and the joy in his dark eyes. And when she gazed inside what had once been a dusty cluttered garage, she saw a remarkable transformation. But it all looked so permanent. She couldn't ignore the sinking feeling in the pit of her stomach.

Everything was there—everything needed for a potter's studio. Cabinets, shelves, an electric kiln in one corner, vented to the outside. The potter's wheel in the middle of the floor. And various potter's tools sitting on surfaces or attached to a Peg-Board hanging on the wall. Even the odor of wet clay coming from a damp closet.

"I'm now a studio production potter," he announced.

She heard the hint of resignation in his tone and thought of the hand-painted pieces on display in her shop. She'd already sold several this week. "You could still be an artist," she said. "You don't have to do intricate hand-painting for your work to be of artistic quality. Why don't you learn some new glazing techniques, or try for distinctive shapes?"

He glared at her, all pleasure gone from his gaze. "I'll be turning out the kind of ware that always sells—the mugs, the bowls, the teapots, the vases. They'll pay the rent and buy the groceries."

She ignored the cold harshness in his eyes and the anger she sensed underlying his restrained tone. "But you have so much talent—too much to waste on becoming just a production potter."

"I can't do the kind of work I used to do," he said. "I told you that."

This time the hard edge to his voice was unmistakable, but she didn't relent. "Then learn a new artistic technique," she countered. "Expand the limits of what you already know."

"I can throw pots and glaze them," he said. "That's what I'm going to do now."

"That's a defeatist attitude. So you've had a little setback. Get up and brush yourself off."

"The accident was more than a little setback. You don't know what you're talking about."

The flare of anger in his dark eyes told her more than his words that something else had happened because of that accident. "Do you want to talk about it?" she asked, softening her voice.

"No! Just drop it."

Instead of intimidating her and sending her scurrying away, his harsh words held her fast. Realizing she'd hit a nerve, she scanned the interior of the garage, groping for a topic of conversation to ease the tension between them.

"You've put a lot of time and money into all this," she said at last, waving her hand toward the shelves and cabinets.

"Just for some of the lumber and fittings," Vince said, his tone still gruff and unyielding, as if he felt he had to defend himself. "Pete and his uncle contributed quite a bit. Pete had already bought the hardware—it was for projects he hadn't gotten to yet. His uncle ran the two-twenty line for the kiln and gave me most of the lumber we used, leftovers from some of his building projects.''

''Very impressive,'' she said, hazarding a glance at his face. His dark eyes no longer sparked with anger.

''Pete's uncle had the saws and other equipment we needed, including the brick-laying stuff. Did you see the kiln outside? He even had the old fire bricks that we used, from a chimney he'd torn down.''

''Another kiln?'' she asked, remembering the sacks of cement and the bricks she'd seen in Pete's truck several days ago when she'd gone home for lunch. Her sense of unease returned.

''For gas-firing,'' he said. ''I can't do everything with one little electric kiln. Come look at this one.'' He led her around to the back of the garage, to a lean-to on a new slab.

''We put it back here,'' he said, ''facing away from the ocean. It had to be outside, because of its size and because of its need for ventilation.''

She stared at the impressive yellow-brick structure. It, too, appeared rather permanent. Her apprehension was increasing by the minute.

''None of this looks at all temporary,'' she said. ''When you asked to rent my garage as a studio, you said you needed a temporary place to work.''

''Uh...I'll have to dismantle everything to move it,'' he said. ''But it can be moved. Pete'll help—when I can afford a place of my own.'' He shrugged. ''Until then, I'll have to work here.''

''Are you ready to start throwing pots?'' she asked. ''Is everything in place?''

"Glad you mentioned it." He looked directly at her. "There's only one more thing I need. A source of hot water."

She sighed. "I guess you can't just run a pipe?"

"It'd be a little more complicated than that. I have an easier solution," he said with uplifted brows. "I don't suppose you'd let me carry water from the laundry tub on your back porch?"

She started to tell him to get his water from the rest room down on the beach, then remembered with a slight feeling of panic that there was only cold water down there.

"Please, Lynn," he added. "I won't disturb you any more than I absolutely have to."

She took a deep breath and expelled it while she pondered this latest attack on her citadel of privacy. "Since I'm gone most of the day," she said, "you'd have to have a key to the back door."

"That shouldn't be a problem." He stared into her eyes. "Or is it?"

The intensity of his gaze pierced her defenses. "All right. I'll get you the spare key."

He followed her to the house and waited on the back porch while she rummaged through a drawer in the kitchen until she found the key.

She held it out to him, then dropped it into the palm of his outstretched hand, without touching him. "But the porch is as far as you go," she said, avoiding his eyes. "I'm locking this door into the kitchen." *Tomorrow,* she added to herself. *As soon as the hardware store opens and I can get a lock.*

He laughed. "Won't that be inconvenient for you, since your bathroom's out here?"

"I'll manage," she said.

He stepped forward, impelled by some force he was only vaguely aware of, and lifted her chin with his fingertips until he was gazing directly into her soft blue eyes. "I don't understand you at all, Lynn Frazer. One minute you're haranguing me, delving for the dark secrets of my past. The next you're erecting a wall to keep me out." He continued to gaze into her eyes, surprised she hadn't turned away or brushed off his hand. And surprised at himself for even daring to touch her.

"Can't we just be friends?" he asked. "Meet on some kind of neutral ground?"

"I was doing just fine until you came along," she murmured, staring back at him.

"And now I'm invading your house, encroaching on your territory and making you uncomfortable." He dropped his hand but maintained the contact with her eyes a moment longer. "What are you afraid of? Me—or yourself?"

Without waiting for her response, he strode from the house, closing the door behind him. He glanced back. Why was he baiting her like that? He didn't need the entanglement any more than she did. But something about her...

He walked straight down the hill, toward the one café in Garrett Cove.

Lynn watched him from the window. She had to admit he'd summed up the situation and the ques-

tions in her own mind admirably. Was it him she was
afraid of? Or her reaction to him? One thing she did
know. He was not the type of man she could ever have
simply as a friend.

He disappeared into the café, where he seemed to be
eating most of his meals when he wasn't at Pete's. She
realized she knew more about his daily activities than
she cared to know.

Why couldn't she get him out of her mind? She
changed from Loafers into sneakers, grabbed her
hooded jacket and headed for the pier.

Once out on the wooden structure, the stiff salty
breeze whipped at her hair until she adjusted and tied
the hood of her jacket, confining the errant strands.
Clouds obscured the horizon and any remaining sun-
light as dusk approached. She took a deep breath or
the bracing air and strolled resolutely to the railing at
the end of the pier, to the one place where she felt
closest to Nick. They'd shared many sunset hours
standing right there, during the two years they were
married.

Grasping the weathered railing, she stared at the
undulating waves. The sea was frothy, but not tumul-
tuous. No waves threatened to engulf the pier this
evening. The only threats were in her mind as her
thoughts strayed from Nick to Vince. She tried to an
alyze what there was about Vince that bothered her
and decided that "bother" was too tame a word to use
to describe the disquieting effects he had on her.

He stirred her interest in a way no man had since
she'd first met Nick. She'd even been dreaming or

Vince—sleeping outside in that van of his, so close yet so far. But they were definitely wrong for each other. They were two people each battling their own demons. And both losing. He couldn't accept the loss of his artistic ability, and she couldn't accept that Nick was truly gone. There was nothing either of them could do for the other.

Darkness closed in, dropping down around her like a cloak, when she realized with a guilty awareness that she'd been thinking far more of Vince than of Nick. She turned around, took three steps and ran into a solid muscular wall.

Vince's arms closed around her, drawing her to him. "Hey, you're going to fall barging around like that."

Her next breath drew in the heady scent of masculinity as he held her tightly against his chest to steady her. She had the overpowering urge to bury her face in his sweatshirt and cling to his strength. Instead, she pushed away from him as if he were fire and she was afraid of being burned.

"Let me go. What are you doing out here?" she demanded, her voice breaking.

"Are you claiming this pier as your private domain?" he asked with a note of irony in his tone.

"I...I..."

"Let me inside that wall you've erected," he said gently. "Maybe I can help you. Your husband is dead, whether you want to admit it or not."

She stared at the dark outlines of his face, barely visible on the cloudy night. How dare he talk to her about something so personal? "I don't need your help.

It's none of your business. Even if it was, there's nothing you can do." She turned away and faced the stiff breeze that stung her cheeks.

"I can offer you comfort," he said behind her, softly. "A shoulder to lean on, someone to talk to."

"No," she said, more loudly than she'd intended. "I have friends, family—if I need them."

"I'd like to be your friend, too." He grasped her arm and pulled her around to face him again. "You offered me a chance to talk a while ago. Now I'm offering you the same chance. Maybe it's what we both need."

"We're complete strangers," she said, twisting away from him again. "It wouldn't work. I've changed my mind."

"You're shutting me out. I've had experience with grief. I . . . I lost a brother a while ago. There were just the two of us."

"You can't help me," she said, glaring at the dark eyes she could barely see. "It would be like the blind leading the blind. You haven't solved your own problems. You're still grieving for the loss of the use of that hand. You've given up art to become nothing but a craftsman."

"I know my physical limits."

She put her hands on her hips and faced him squarely. "And I'll grieve in my own way. Please, leave me alone. Go away. I don't want you here." She stomped her foot, a muffled sound against the roar of the waves.

"All right. If that's what you want. Live with your ghost." He stalked away down the pier.

She couldn't watch him go. Despite what she'd told him, she *was* no longer sure what she wanted. Turning to the sea for solace, the dark watery depths drew her gaze. "Oh, Nick. What do I do now?" she whispered to the waves.

She stood there, staring at the sea, for what seemed an eternity until she was certain Vince had had enough time to get off the pier and up the hill. Then she turned and started home.

He was standing under the lone streetlight.

She walked off the pier and started to go past him. Then she stopped.

He was leaning against the post, watching her. Something was nagging at him, telling him that Lynn needed his help, despite her reluctance to admit it.

She brushed back her hood, letting her blond hair fly in the breeze. "Give it up, Vince."

"Give what up?"

"Whatever it is you're trying to do."

"I'm just trying to talk to you." He squared his shoulders and closed the gap between them. "What is it you expect to find out on the end of the pier?"

"How do you come up with such stupid questions?" Her tone was brusque and unyielding. She started walking and he fell into step beside her.

"It's not a stupid question if it has an answer." He glanced at her, but she kept her eyes straight ahead.

"When I'm out there, I feel as if Nick is with me." Her words were low, half muffled by the sounds of the ocean behind them.

They started up the path to the house. "Wouldn't you be happier with a flesh-and-blood man?"

"No!" she almost shouted. "No one can take Nick's place."

"That isn't what I meant. But you can love again. A person doesn't have only one chance at love in a lifetime."

"I could never love anyone else until I know for sure that Nick is dead."

He heard the fierce determination in her voice and found himself feeling sorry for anyone who had the misfortune to fall in love with her. "You are undoubtedly the most stubborn female I've ever encountered."

"And you are the most relentless male I have ever come across."

"There are times, like right now, that I wish Pete had never talked me into coming out to Garrett Cove."

She looked up at him. "And I wish you had never come. You do know what Pete is trying to do, don't you?"

"What?"

"He's playing matchmaker. I think he has some mistaken idea that you and I would be good for each other."

They had reached her back door. Without a backward glance, she walked into the house and disappeared from view.

He went to the garage and let himself in with his key. What she'd said made sense. No wonder Pete wanted him to ask her for the use of her garage. Pete *had* set him up. And baited him. Telling him that Lynn had been grieving and in a depressed state for a year and a half, telling him that everyone was so worried about her. That damn Pete knew he wouldn't be able to resist such a challenge. Pete knew he'd tangle with her over the grief thing.

He dropped down on a stool and felt his anger rising. He wasn't looking for a woman—for a relationship. That was the last thing in the world he needed now. But he'd like to help her—without getting involved.

Then a little voice asked him, *If you're not interested in her, why are you so angry?* He had to stop and think about that one. Was it more than just feeling sorry for her? After all, he knew what she was going through.

Then another thought struck him. If he was going to get involved with a woman, and it was a big "if," Lynn Frazer would be a likely choice. How did Pete know that?

He walked back outside. The light in the kitchen beckoned to him. Through the sheer curtain he could see Lynn moving about, probably fixing her dinner. He frowned. She was a pixie of a woman who didn't realize how sexy and desirable she was. Firm uplifted breasts teased at the front of her sweater. Small shapely lips drew into a sultry pout. And the way she tossed that long blond hair of hers behind her shoulders . . . He felt a stirring in his loins.

He knocked on the back door and saw her face peer through the window at him. She opened the door a crack. "What do you want now?" Her tone accused rather than questioned.

"Just to tell you I won't bother you anymore with unsolicited advice," he said. "I think you're right. If Pete really is trying to set us up, he's got the wrong two people. It would never work."

She frowned and he saw a flicker of something in the depths of her eyes that puzzled him.

"Good night," he said, and headed back to the garage. They were all wrong for each other, he told himself again. Too many problems. Now he just had to convince himself of that.

Four

A brisk morning breeze caressed Lynn's hair and face as she started down the driveway toward her shop. Loud cursing coming from the garage broke into her meandering thoughts. She stopped next to the garage and heard a loud thumping sound followed by more cursing.

Her curiosity aroused, she peered through the window and gasped. She knocked, but Vince didn't acknowledge her presence. Pulling open the door, she stepped inside just as he hurled a misshapen bowl against the wall. Several other lumps of wet clay littered the floor along with items that had fallen off their hooks on the Peg-Board.

"Are you all right?" she asked tentatively, not sure she should say anything after their encounter last night. But he'd said he wanted to be a friend. He'd said he would keep his opinions to himself. She ventured closer.

He rose from the stool, and the scowl on his face as he turned to her spoke volumes. "Can't get my rhythm going this morning, that's all. It's been a long time since I've thrown a pot."

She stifled a giggle. "Looks to me like you're throwing quite well." She gestured toward the scattered lumps of clay. "You're letting your anger take over and add to your stress, you know. You'll never do a decent piece that way."

"And I suppose you have a solution?"

"Sit down," she commanded.

He lowered himself onto the stool behind the wheel and quirked one brow. Without thinking of the possible consequences of what she was doing, she walked around behind him and grasped his shoulders, slowly massaging the tense muscles beneath her fingers—the same way she'd always done for Nick when he'd come home from a day of fishing, his shoulders knotted from hefting the heavy poles.

The heat from Vince's body radiated through the thin turtleneck shirt he wore. She inhaled the subtle aroma of maleness that mingled with the earthy odor of wet clay permeating the room. A day's growth of beard shadowed his face. Steadfastly ignoring the pulses of desire skittering uninvited through her body, she continued her rhythmic kneading of his shoulder muscles. She could feel him begin to relax under her ministrations. She couldn't stop now. It wouldn't do to let him know how being close to him, touching him, was affecting her.

She'd been too long without a man. That was all it was. But then she brushed that thought aside. She had to admit there was something special about Vince, something that stirred her blood and made her glad she was a woman. But she wasn't going to act on any insane impulses. She couldn't. Not when there was still a chance Nick could come back. She glanced at her wedding band. Until she knew for sure that Nick was dead, she would not take it off.

A sigh escaped Vince's lips as he twisted around. "You have a magic touch," he said, his tone indicating a much more relaxed state of mind than when she'd entered the garage. "I feel better already."

She stepped away from him, anxious to break the physical contact.

He dipped his clay-streaked hands into a bucket of water and then wiped them dry. Grinning self-consciously, he said, "You're right. Beating myself up isn't going to solve anything."

He stared at her a moment, then took a step nearer. She could see a glint of desire shimmering in his eyes. Mesmerized by the power he emanated, she didn't move when he grasped her shoulders and pulled her close.

His mouth hovered so near she could feel his warm breath. It seemed an eternity before his lips finally covered hers, hungrily exploring. The touch of his lips sent tendrils of need spiraling through her. She leaned into him, kissing him back, no thought of resistance entering her mind.

When he broke the contact with her lips, his gaze continued to hold her eyes captive. "I'm sorry," he said quietly. "I shouldn't have done that."

He released her and turned away, his shoulders and chest heaving. He stared into the corner of the garage, hoping she'd take the hint and leave. It wouldn't do for her to see just how much that kiss had affected him.

Why had he done it? Because he wanted to. That answer was easy enough. He'd wanted to taste her lips for days. What surprised him was her response, her participation. Surprised and puzzled him.

He heard the door close behind him. When he turned around, she was gone. Only the lingering scent of flowers from the fragrance she wore told him she'd been there. He stood by the window in the door and watched her slowly walk down the hill toward her shop.

Lynn turned around when she reached the bottom of the hill and looked back toward the garage. She could just make out Vince's head and shoulders at the window.

Her own heart still beat wildly. She watched him for a moment, wondering why she hadn't tried to stop him from kissing her. She knew she had to get over losing her husband before becoming involved with another man. Wasn't that the way things worked? With a sigh of frustration she strode quickly on to her shop.

By the time she opened the door she'd resolved again not to get involved with Vince Coulter—or any man.

Several times that morning she caught herself running her fingers over her lips as she relived that devastating kiss and felt the stirrings in her body the memory evoked. He'd said he was sorry. What did he mean by that? She preferred to think he was sorry he'd lost control. Just as she had. Her own response was every bit as incriminating. Maybe *she* should have apologized to *him*. She smiled at the thought.

Then a frown wrinkled her brow. Where did they go from here? She refused to dwell on the question.

The kiss was a mistake. She was sure of it. Twisting her wedding band on her finger, she vowed she wouldn't allow it to happen again. By touching him in the first place, intimately massaging his tense shoulders, she'd brought it on. Maybe she could explain to him . . . No, forget the explanations, she told herself. Just don't get into that kind of situation again.

By lunchtime she was convinced the kiss was an accident that wouldn't be repeated. All she had to do was avoid touching him again. She passed by the garage on the way to her house without longing to go in. When she opened the back door of the house and stepped into the porch, she noticed the unmistakable scent of shaving lotion still lingering in the air. He'd come into the house while she was gone and used the bathroom to shave.

Her first impulse was a sense of outrage that he'd dared to use her bathroom without her permission. Then guilt set in. How selfish she was, making him use the rest room down on the beach, with its icy-cold water, when her own little house was arranged with the bathroom conveniently located on the back porch. He already had the key to the porch. The latch she'd installed on the kitchen door would keep him out of the rest of the house.

Before she lost her nerve, she marched out the back door and straight to the garage. Vince was bent over the wheel molding a vase when she opened the door, walking right in without knocking.

He turned at the sound and a smile softened his features.

"I've decided to be neighborly," she said. "You can use the bathroom in my house. Just clean up after yourself. I don't provide maid service." With that, she hastily retreated.

Vince heard a timid knock on the garage door a few days later. "Come in," he called without looking up from the half-finished vase on the wheel.

He maintained his concentration on the evolving piece, slowly guiding the clay upward with his hands to fashion the neck and the rim of the vessel. Only as he was cutting the piece from the wheel did he allow himself to know that it was Lynn who'd come through the door.

What amused him was how her knock was always so tentative, as if she wasn't sure she should disturb him. The only time she'd come in without knocking was when she'd announced he could use her bathroom. He could feel her presence hovering behind him now. As she moved closer, he breathed in the delicate scent of her floral fragrance. Was it lavender? No. A subtle blend of some kind, he decided.

"You're making progress," Lynn said.

He spun the stool around and felt that tingle of awareness she awakened in him whenever he was close to her. She stopped in front of the shelves along the side wall, gazing at the rows of drying ware.

"I'll bisque-fire the first batch in a couple of days," he said. "Then we'll see what kind of progress I've made. It's been so long since I've thrown any pots I'm not so sure they'll hold up in the kiln."

"They look fine to me," she said. Then she spotted a pitcher on top of the damp cupboard and picked it up to examine it more closely. "Don't put this one back into the clay," she said. "Look at the distinctive shape. Look at the lines. It may not be as straight as normal functional ware, but there's a certain symmetry about it. I like it." She smiled a soft wistful smile.

"But it's not the kind of thing I'm attempting to do," he said, letting his voice show his exasperation.

"I know," she said quietly. "It's better. Somehow this one speaks to me."

He scowled. "You don't know what you're talking about."

"With the right glazing techniques," she said, "this pitcher could go in a gallery, instead of a craft shop, and outsell ten of your other pieces." She waved a hand toward the assortment of functional pottery on the shelves.

"But what if I can't get the right glaze on it?" he asked, his tone decidedly negative. "Then what do I have? A piece of junk only fit for the trash."

"I'm not saying the first piece you do will be a big success," she replied. "I'm only suggesting you try.

Do a little experimenting. That's what you're doing, anyway—experimenting with becoming a craftsman."

The words stung. He was aware of his own rising anger. "And you're not sure I can make it."

She stood in front of him, hands on her hips. "I never said that. Those thoughts are in *your* mind. You're the one giving up on yourself. Have a little faith."

He heard the challenge in her voice and fought back with the one weapon he had. "You're a great one to talk," he said. "You're giving up on life itself, hiding behind a dead husband, unable to get past a day without communing with him from the end of that damn pier."

"I don't go there every day," she said, her anger flaring.

"Just about," he replied. "And you're still wearing your wedding band. Someday you're going to have to accept his death and get on with your life."

"It's no concern of yours."

"And the kind of pottery I choose to make is a concern of yours?" he asked. "You sell pottery made by other craftsmen all the time."

She drew a breath as if to calm herself, and faced him directly. "The potters and I both make more money when the work is original," she said. "When it has that spark that says the person who made it is a creator breathing life into his designs."

"But a mistake isn't an artistic creation." He was almost shouting.

"You're the one who labeled this intriguing pitcher a mistake," she said, looking it over again as she held it carefully in her hands. Then she set it back down and stepped away with a thoughtful look on her face. "I say there's still a lot more artistic potential in you than you care to acknowledge." She punctuated her words with a nod of her head.

"I don't have the control I used to have," he said, angry at himself and at her for daring to point out to him his lack of will. "I can't do it." He stood up. "Get out of here. Leave me alone."

"You're scared. Admit it. You're scared." She lifted her chin and glared at him.

"All right, I admit it. I'm scared stiff I won't be able to make a living doing what I love to do." He glared right back. "Now are you satisfied? Now will you go away and leave me alone?"

"Okay. I'll go. Just don't throw away that pitcher." She marched out the door, slamming it behind her hard enough to rattle the window.

He picked up the pitcher, and the temptation to hurl it against the wall was almost overwhelming.

After a few deep breaths to bring his anger under control, he held the pitcher at arm's length, letting his artist's eye really look at it. Its squat irregular shape reminded him of a gourd. The bottom was flat, but the angle of the spout a bit skewed....

He set the pitcher on the turning wheel and worked with the lip for a few minutes, molding it, smoothing it, building it up in one thin place and working out the excess clay in another. A glimmer of excitement skittered through him.

Maybe she was right—about this one. Maybe the right glaze—a smooth, burnished surface perhaps? Like bronze.

He worked with the piece for a while longer, his enthusiasm mounting. At last satisfied that the pitcher had some potential, he set it on the shelf with the other pieces waiting for the kiln.   After rinsing his hands in a bucket of water and drying them, he put on his jacket. The least he could do was apologize for shouting at her and sending her away.

Once out the door, he glanced down the hill toward the ocean and caught sight of a slim figure at the end of the pier. A sinking feeling coiled in the pit of his stomach. Communing with her dead husband again. Hiding from life. He turned back to the garage.

Then he stopped and swiveled around to face the ocean again. The realization hit him that he needed to talk to her, needed her to understand why he felt the way he did. That meant explaining to her what had happened back East on Long Island. Was he ready to tell her the whole truth? Or only part of it? Why had she become so important to him?

It wasn't just a physical attraction, either. Otherwise he wouldn't care how she felt. He wouldn't be upset that he'd sent her away in anger. And he wouldn't care that she was wasting her life waiting for some kind of sign that her husband was really dead.

Had the invincible Vince Coulter, a man who'd never considered a woman as necessary to his happiness, finally fallen in love, and with someone who couldn't let go of the memory of her dead husband? How could he compete with a ghost, especially when he had ghosts of his own?

Five

Lynn had no sooner returned from the pier and closed the kitchen door behind her when she heard the outer door open. Glancing over her shoulder through the window, she saw Vince stride to the inner door and open it, boldly walking into the kitchen. Her pulse quickened, his angry outburst earlier still very much on her mind. "I didn't say you could come in here."

"You going to throw me out?" he challenged.

She kept her voice calm while trying to assess his current mood. "If you've come to argue."

"I came to apologize for shouting at you," he said. "I know you were just trying to help."

She sighed. With this volatile man she never knew what to expect. "Apology accepted. Is that all?"

"Yes," he said. "No."

She waited, wondering at the apprehension in his eyes.

"Look, I..." He shrugged and backed away. "It doesn't matter. See you tomorrow."

"Wait," she said. Something puzzling in the expression on his face intrigued her. She made an instant decision. "Join me for dinner. We can talk."

He glanced around the kitchen, undoubtedly for signs of a meal in preparation. "The food's in the refrigerator, and I can just heat it up," she said, gesturing toward the microwave. "It'll be ready in a jiffy."

The beginning of a smile tipped the corners of his mouth. "I'll wash up."

By the time he returned to the kitchen she'd set the small table in the nook and the tantalizing aroma of hot fried chicken filled the room. She saw the pleased look on his face as she added potato salad from the refrigerator and a steaming bowl of baked beans from the microwave.

"Smells delicious," he said, taking the chair she indicated.

"Do you drink milk?" she asked, suddenly aware that there were many things about him she didn't know.

"Milk's fine."

She poured two glasses and set them on the table. "Help yourself," she said, trying to disguise just how nervous she was having him here. Whatever had possessed her to invite him into the intimacy of her small kitchen? He filled the room with his presence. She speared a chicken leg, then took salad and beans, willing herself to relax.

Why should she feel so uncomfortable sharing a meal with Vince? She'd known him almost two weeks, she'd been in his studio, they'd talked many times, yet this was the first time he'd been farther than the back porch. Had she been purposely keeping him outside?

Of course she had. Because he wasn't Nick. Because he was a man she was attracted to. Because she couldn't get him out of her mind, day or night.

"How long have you lived in Garrett Cove?" he asked, breaking into her troubled thoughts.

She raised her eyes to his and saw a strange sparkle. He was as nervous as she was! "Nick was living here in town when I married him—three and a half years ago. I was born just over in San Luis Obispo."

"And you intend to stay here?"

"Yes," she replied emphatically. "I could never leave here. Not after all that's happened."

"I didn't think I'd ever leave Long Island, either," he said with a frown. "And here I find myself on the other side of the continent."

"Wouldn't it have been easier to start over with supportive friends and family around you?" She thought of her own family and how hard they had tried to help her.

"No," he replied. "Just the opposite. My friends on Long Island either pitied me or told me I could still do the same kind of work as before, if only I tried harder. I couldn't tolerate those attitudes."

"And your family felt the same?"

"My father, a businessman to the core, always insisted I'd never make a decent living as an artist," he said, then hesitated. "He was the first one to say 'I told you so' after the accident."

She saw the haunted look in his eyes. "You couldn't help what happened to you," she said. "An accident is an accident."

His expression was tight with strain. "The accident was all my fault," he said, emphasizing the word "accident." He took a deep breath before going on. "I was clowning around, not paying attention to my driving. We'd just come from a gallery opening that was supposed to herald a momentous step in an illustrious career. You know the Greek theory of hubris—the gods shoot you down when you get too cocky? I clipped a guardrail and ran off the road that night, broadsiding a tree. Utter stupidity on my part!"

"And you haven't let yourself forget it for a minute," she added. "When are you going to forgive yourself?"

"Never. I'll live with the consequences of that night for the rest of my life. My brother died in the accident."

He glanced away. She felt the anguish in his words and just stared at him, at a complete loss as to how to respond.

Then he pulled up his sleeve and thrust his arm forward. A six-inch jagged scar, like a bolt of lightning, flared on his inner wrist, its ruddy hue setting it apart from the surrounding flesh. "This is my punishment for killing my brother."

She reached out and covered the scar with her hand. "You haven't dealt with your own grief, yet you're telling me to let go of mine."

"Oh, but I have dealt with it. I'm getting on with my life." He pulled his arm away from her hand. "Now that I've discovered I can still throw pots, I know I can support myself making pottery. I can mix the glazes and do whatever else needs to be done."

She couldn't resist an additional jab. "And see the potential in design. That slice on your wrist didn't sever the connections to your brain."

"I don't want to be an artist anymore, just a potter."

"Don't close yourself off from what you could be. Build a new life. A better one."

"I don't deserve anything more than what I'm aiming for. I need an income now. Besides, it takes time to develop the skills to make an artistic statement. I don't have that kind of time."

He'd said the words without the anger she'd expected. With a resignation that saddened her. She got up from the table and took a check from her purse in the living room, handing it to him. "I intended to give this to you earlier—before you ran me out of the garage. It's the first installment on the rest of your life. I've already sold a fourth of those pieces of yours."

His eyes widened as he stared at the check. "Almost enough to pay Pete back what I borrowed from him." He glanced up at her. "Uh...I haven't yet paid you any rent on the garage."

"Pay Pete first," she said. "One other thing. I've noticed you're not taking the time to go down to the café for lunch. I'll leave a sandwich and fruit in my refrigerator for you. You can come get it when you're hungry."

"You don't have to do that," he said.

"I want to. Can't have a starving artist on my hands. I'll leave the kitchen door unlocked." But only during the day, she added to herself. "You can put drinks, anything else you want, in the refrigerator too."

The haunted look left his face. A half smile softened his features. In that moment her impression of him changed. He was handsome, in his own unique manner. Besides being overtly masculine, in a tantalizing way.

How had he managed to become a part of her life in such a short time? She *cared* what happened to him. She cared that he hadn't exorcised his demons.

And he stirred delicious feelings deep inside her that should never be.

"Do you ever take a day off?" Vince asked, reaching for another piece of chicken.

His question surprised her, and she hesitated a moment before answering. "No, I don't. I keep my shop open seven days a week." She watched his eyes while he weighed her answer.

One brow lifted quizzically. "What if you're sick?"

"I post a sign in the window and go back to bed." She pursed her lips. "It doesn't happen very often."

"I think you ought to put a sign in the window tomorrow and play hooky, show me some of the countryside, like that rugged coastal area to the north." He gazed at her expectantly.

"I can't."

"You mean you won't." His eyes challenged. "What are you afraid of?"

"I'm not afraid of anything."

"Then go for a drive with me." He picked up the check she'd given him and waved it at her. "Pete doesn't get *every* penny of this. I'll buy us lunch along the way."

She met his even gaze. "I'll think about it. I haven't taken a day off in months."

And she did think about it—constantly—all the rest of the evening. And changed her mind countless times until she had to admit that she was afraid. Afraid of him. Afraid of the feelings he aroused in her. Yet . . . what would be so wrong with spending a day with him? She hadn't done anything simply for the fun of it in a long time.

About ten o'clock she clicked off the television movie she'd only half watched and heard Vince running water in the bathroom. She waited, listening for him to leave the house. Instead, she heard a knock on the kitchen door.

When she turned the latch and opened the door, he grinned at her. "I filled the van with gas tonight. Put your sign in the window and be ready to leave by nine in the morning." He turned and strode out the door toward the van parked by the garage.

She realized she had several choices. She could run after him and tell him she wasn't going. She could tell him in the morning when he came looking for her. Or she could go with him. Her traitorous heart made the decision.

The maroon van sped north on the coastal highway, a twisting, narrow, two-lane road built by convict labor between the two world wars. Lynn entertained Vince with stories of some of the local history as he drove. At least by keeping to neutral subjects she hoped to avoid the topics that sparked too personal a conversation. For a reason she wasn't ready to analyze, she wanted simply to enjoy this day and friendly company.

As she gazed at Vince's rugged profile, she realized there was one thing she was thankful for. In the van the two bucket seats in the front were far enough apart that their arms wouldn't accidently touch. In her little Honda they would have been sitting much closer together. Then Lynn glanced behind the seats. Vince's rumpled sleeping bag lay on a mattress. She felt a tightening in her chest. They were driving up the highway in his bedroom.

"I didn't tell you why I wanted to take a day off today," Vince said, breaking into her thoughts. "I fired the first batch of pottery. They're cooling right now. When we get back, we'll open the kiln. Then we'll see what kind of a potter I am."

"You're nervous," she said, the truth dawning on her. "Are these the first ones you've done since the accident?"

"Oh, I tried to throw some pots before I had the strength back in my wrist," he said. "What a mistake. They were utter failures."

"This time you decided you were ready," she said.

"I worked with a physical therapist for a while, until my money was almost gone." He sighed, keeping his eyes on the winding road. "That's when I knew I had to get away and make a new start somewhere else. So I called Pete and talked to him. He'd suggested before that I come to Garrett Cove."

"So Pete encouraged you to come," she put in.

"He told me about the summer crowds on the beach. About the nearby golf course and those big motels. And about your shop and how well pottery sold there." He paused. "He did keep one bit of information from me, though. He didn't tell me how pretty you were."

She was glad he had to keep his eyes on the winding road and couldn't see the flush in her cheeks. Somewhere back in her mind, a little voice reminded her she was making a mistake coming with him. She refused to listen.

The road was climbing again, from a stretch at sea level back to a high promontory, and she realized where they were. "There's a great view up ahead," she said.

He pulled the van off the highway and stopped short of the low rock wall. She climbed out and walked over to the wall, the sun shining from a cloudless sky, a stiff breeze blowing her hair into her face. She felt rather than saw him at her side. Concentrating, instead, on the scene below, she gazed down at the steep, brush-covered slope that dropped to the swirling gray-green water. The rocks jutting from the surf were surrounded by frothy white foam. Occasionally a cascading spray broke into the air with an iridescent shimmer. Gulls hovering overhead, drifting in the breeze, squawked out a warning. She breathed the clean ocean air and savored its salty twang.

"Too bad we can't get down there for a closer look," he said. "It's beautiful. So wild."

She smiled at the almost worshipful look on his face. His artistic sensibility was engaged. He might just do better here on the Coast, with new places to see and new artists to inspire him. He needed to meet the other artists in the area, too. She had a few contacts. She'd have to see to it sometime.

When they returned to the van, he opened the passenger door for her and grasped her arm to help her in. She felt the heat of his hand through the fabric of her sweater, just a gentle touch that radiated warmth to all parts of her body. Her eyes met his and he turned away, closing the door.

They ate their lunch at a roadside café before going in search of another promontory from which to view the ocean. They found one about twenty miles north. No other cars were there when Vince steered the van off the highway.

Lynn shivered as the breeze from the ocean tugged at her. An uneasy feeling crept over her. Vince had been unusually quiet during lunch, and he had looked at her with a warmth that had made her tingle all over. Now they were alone.

"Come on," he said, grabbing her hand and pulling her over the low rock wall and around some large boulders. She knew she shouldn't go with him, but couldn't stop herself. They found a trail that led to a spot out of sight of the highway, tucked behind an outcropping of rock and brush. The rains of the previous weeks had left a carpet of new green grass among the low bushes dotting the hillside.

She glanced back at the trail, then at Vince. Smiling, he pulled her toward him. The look in his eyes told her it wasn't the ocean that interested him.

"I don't think this is a good idea," she said, shaking her head to reinforce her words.

"I do," he whispered against her lips just before his mouth touched hers in a slow sensuous assault that seemed to go on and on. Powerless to stop him, her lips parted, granting him entrance, and he deepened the kiss, his arms crushing her to him, molding her body against his.

A kaleidoscope of conflicting emotions raged through her as she felt the hard evidence of his need. She wanted his kisses, wanted to feel his arms around her. Her heart beat wildly and ripples of desire consumed her as she returned his kisses, giving in to the delectable whirling sensations of her own need.

Yet it was wrong, all wrong. Her mind knew that. But her body wasn't paying any attention. She couldn't bring herself to give up the warmth of his lips and the heated awareness of his body clasped against hers.

She felt momentarily bereft when he pulled away from her and lowered her to the ground, where the scent of grass mingled with the salty air and tickled her nostrils.

The weight of his body pressed against hers as he lay half on top of her, his mouth joining with hers again. She gave in to her aching need and returned the fervor of his kisses.

It was only when his hand slipped under her sweater, hot against her cool flesh, exploring and finding the swollen peak of her breast beneath her bra that her reason began to assert itself. If Nick wasn't dead, she was still married.

She pushed against Vince's chest, turning her head away from the magic of his kiss. "No...no. Please stop."

He pulled back. "Are you sure that's what you want?" he said, his deep voice husky with passion.

"Yes." She didn't trust herself to say any more. Sitting up, she turned away from him and adjusted her bra and smoothed her sweater.

"Why?"

"You know why," she said, raising her eyes to his. What she saw alarmed her.

His pupils were dilated with anger. "No, I don't. I thought you were enjoying it as much as I was." The words came out in a bitter torrent. He grasped her arm and pulled her around to face him. "We'd be good together. Can't you see that?'' He was almost shouting.

She cowered under the verbal onslaught. "No! I shouldn't have come with you today. I'm . . . I'm not ready for this."

"How many years is it going to take before you are?" His voice was low and hard. He stood up, towering over her. "You could let go of Nick and get on with your own life. You're young and beautiful and desirable. Don't hide away with nothing but memories."

She saw the hurt in his eyes and knew she'd let things go too far. Too far for both of them. "You don't understand. I can't stop loving him just because he's gone. I feel such guilt each time I let you touch me or kiss me."

"Guilt?" He snorted derisively. "You've done nothing to feel guilty about. Your husband is dead. Dead and gone."

"You're being cruel. You of all people ought to know the power of guilt. You haven't given up your guilt over your brother's death."

"But I caused the accident that killed Damon. You didn't capsize your husband's fishing boat." He reached down and pulled her to her feet. "Let's get out of here." He released her hands and headed off down the trail toward the van. She followed him, brushing at the grass and twigs caught on her sweater and jeans.

On the drive back to Garrett Cove all her attempts at casual conversation were met with either silence or monosyllabic replies. She wanted to say something to ease the tension between them, but there wasn't anything that hadn't already been said. He didn't understand her feelings, probably never would. She hardly understood them herself. One thing she did know. Her own unfulfilled longing clamored for release. But that's all it was—a physical need. It couldn't be anything else.

Vince parked the van in its usual spot beside the garage. "I'm going to open the kiln," he said without looking at her. "You can come watch if you want."

She almost told him no, then decided that would be childish. She followed him through the side door into the garage, her mind and body in utter confusion. Fighting an overwhelming urge to touch him, she stopped several feet behind him and waited.

"I did the firing yesterday afternoon and evening," he said, his tone devoid of its earlier anger, "then cracked the door slightly before we left." He didn't say anything else as he opened the door of the kiln fully and began taking the pieces from the shelves, one by one, and setting them on a nearby bench.

He turned toward her with the squat gourdlike pitcher in his hand. "You were right. It does have potential." His eyes met hers for the first time since their disastrous encounter up the coast. They were still and dark—no anger, no passion.

She began to relax. "Now what will you do with it?"

"I have an idea that'll give it a unique finish. If it works, I'll show you when it comes out of the final firing." He set the pitcher on the bench and took the last of the pottery from the kiln.

"Did everything come out okay?" She surveyed the pieces on the bench. "What kind of glazes are you planning on using with this batch?"

"I'm going to experiment with several kinds I've never used before and find out what works the best," he said. "I've gotten this far. I threw the pots and fired them once. Now I go on to the next step. Then we'll see what kind of production potter I am."

He said the words without any air of confidence. He was scared—scared he wouldn't make it as a production potter. And she was pushing him to be even more. She wanted to put her arms around him and reassure him that he'd do just fine, that he had the skills and talent. But putting her arms around him was impossible now. From now on her goal had to be keeping a safe distance between them. If only he'd cooperate.

He faced her directly. "The next firing will be the crucial one. The real test. After I get the glazes on."

"You can do it," she said. "I have faith in you." She watched his eyes, wondering how those dark depths that were blazing with desire such a short time ago could now look so cold.

"One more thing before you go," he said. "I want to apologize for today. I was out of line."

She looked up at him. "And I apologize for not stopping you sooner."

He frowned. "I should have listened to you when you said it wasn't a good idea. But I thought I could change your mind. And I thought I had myself under control, that I'd be able to stop with a few kisses. I had no intention of going as far as I did, of forcing myself on you.''

She stared at him, not sure what to say.

"I came here to make pottery, not to make love. I got sidetracked. I won't let it happen again." His words were uttered without emotion. And they drove through her like a razor-sharp sword.

Six

The door swished shut behind a departing customer, and Lynn glanced up at the clock. Almost closing time. She sighed. Maybe she ought to stop by the garage on her way to the house. See if Vince needed anything.

She hadn't seen much of him at all in the week since their drive up the coast. He was avoiding her, getting up earlier than she did in the morning. By the time she'd stumbled into the bathroom for her wake-up shower, he'd already been there, the scent of his soap and shaving lotion lingering in the moist air. He seemed to time his arrivals and departures to not coincide with hers. Deliberately. And it hurt.

And she'd stayed out of the garage on purpose. Avoiding him as he avoided her.

Thirty minutes later a shadow fell across the floor. She looked up in surprise to see Vince standing just outside the door, as if hesitating to come in.

She waited, her pulses fluttering.

He opened the door and crossed to her, holding out a bronze-tone pitcher like an offering. It was the squat little pitcher he'd wanted to throw away. She smiled and took it from him, setting it on the shelf in front of her. Then she stepped back and gazed at it. "I love it," she said reverently.

"Now we'll see if it'll sell," he said, his own voice full of skepticism.

"It will. I guarantee it."

"I'll bring the rest of the first batch tomorrow." He grinned sheepishly. "But I couldn't wait to show you this one."

"I'm glad." She smiled and gazed at the pitcher again. It was perfect, as she'd known it would be. When she turned back to Vince, he'd gone.

The next morning he was back.

"Hi," was her simple greeting, but her tone was soft, welcoming.

He answered with a grunt and set a box on the floor. She opened the lid and saw an assortment of vases, bowls, cups, pitchers—the kind of ware she got regularly from other production potters.

After bringing in a second box from his van out front, he approached her. "This is it," he said. "The ones that are worth selling."

"No more little bronze-tone pitchers?" She glanced at the pitcher on the top shelf of the display table that sat in the middle of the room.

"That's one of a kind. There won't be any more." He snapped out the words.

"You're not going to try to make any more distinctive pieces." It was a flat statement. She knew the answer. His words and attitude was unmistakable.

"I'm a production potter," he replied with a scowl. "I told you that. That's the best I can do now." He laughed—a deep, throaty, mocking sound. "That pitcher was nothing more than a lucky accident, not likely to ever be repeated."

She stared at him. "I don't believe you. You've done it once. You can do it again."

"Believe what you want," he said bitterly. "But I know what kind of pottery I'm going to make."

She leaned against the counter and suddenly felt very reckless, ready to challenge him again. "You're trying to punish yourself by denying your abilities. What you suffered in that accident was punishment enough."

"You don't know what you're talking about."

She pursed her lips. "Oh, but I do. I talked to Pete a couple of days ago. He told me you took the full brunt of the impact when you broadsided that tree, that you had a broken leg, cuts and bruises, and a head injury that had you on the critical list for days."

"I got what I deserved." He strode toward the door.

She called after him, "Pete also said that there were four of you in that car, all clowning around." He turned and glared at her. "If your brother had been wearing a seat belt like the rest of you, he wouldn't have been thrown from the car and he wouldn't have been killed. The other two passengers had only very minor injuries."

He stood at the door, one hand on the knob. "He might still have died. He was in the front seat beside me."

She advanced toward him. "Damon lived on the edge, tempting fate all the time. He refused to ever wear a seat belt. Pete said that, too. Your brother's life-style is not your fault. You didn't kill him. You don't have to punish yourself with guilt for the rest of your life."

"But I was driving the car!"

She kept her own voice under tight control. "Did you tell him to put on a seat belt?"

"Yeah—though I knew it wouldn't do any good."

She suppressed her urge to smile. "His refusal to wear a seat belt made his death his own fault. Not yours."

"But I caused the accident. He died. It has to be my fault."

"You're using your guilt as an excuse. You're not letting yourself be what you're capable of being." She put her hands on her hips and faced him squarely.

He towered over her, scowling. "Maybe I am. But it's my guilt. And I do know my limitations."

"I know your potential. I can see it in that bronze-tone pitcher."

"You're weaving fantasies." He marched out of the shop and climbed into his van without a backward glance.

She stared after him. Vince Coulter was not willing to take any risks. His damaged ego was too fragile right now. She stewed about it for the rest of the morning, then formulated a plan. She'd show that man what a lucky accident was worth!

Lynn slit open the envelope and took out the check, hardly glancing at the note that accompanied it. A huge smile of satisfaction spread across her face. She stuffed the check into the pocket of her windbreaker, pulled a chilled bottle of champagne from the refrigerator and uncorked it, then picked up two goblets and raced out to the garage.

She pushed open the door without knocking and surprised Vince as he was loading the kiln. He glowered at her at first, then saw the champagne bottle. His brows shot up. "What's going on?"

"We're going to celebrate," she said, setting the goblets on a table and pouring the champagne. She handed him a glass, then the check. Then she raised her own glass. "To your future."

He stared at the check, frowned and looked up at her. "What's all this about? I never sold anything to the Irvington Gallery in Los Angeles."

She grinned. "Yes, you did," she said. "That bronze-tone pitcher. Your 'lucky accident.'"

"You sent it to this gallery?" he asked.

"And they sold it in two days for ten times what I could have sold it for in my shop," she said triumphantly.

Vince shrugged. "This doesn't prove a thing." He set the glass down without tasting the wine. "Selling that pitcher was only another lucky accident," he said with a frown.

"You can make more pieces like that." She raised her goblet in a salute and took a sip. "The owner of the gallery is a friend of mine. She agreed with me that the pitcher was top quality. That it had a character all its own.''

''I can't count on lucky accidents to support myself.''

''I disagree. If you've done it once, you can do it again.''

''Why'd you send it down there?''

''Two reasons. Because I knew it would bring more money in the gallery—'' she smiled sheepishly ''—and to get temptation out of my way. I didn't dare keep it around. I was tempted to buy it for myself, but I couldn't afford to pay that kind of money for it.'' She indicated the check he held in his hand. ''I had to get the thing out of my shop while I still could.''

She watched his eyes, wishing she knew what he was feeling right now. His expression, she decided, was one of bewilderment more than anything else.

''Thank you,'' he said, picking up the goblet, ''for believing in me when I couldn't believe in myself. You've given me something I didn't have before. Hope.'' He clinked his glass against hers. ''Here's to the future.''

She smiled, glad he was beginning to see the potential he still had as an artist. But a little cloud passed through her mind. What if he *did* make it? What if he became as famous on the West Coast as he'd been on Long Island? Would he leave Garrett Cove? Did she want him to?

Vince paced the garage, glancing out the window every couple of minutes to see if any lights were on, indicating Lynn was up. He had to talk to her. It had been a week since she'd given him the check from the gallery, a week of soul-searching and experimenting for him.

But his conversation with Pete the evening before was what had him upset this morning. He'd stewed about it half the night. Now he had the ammunition to get back at her, and by golly he was going to use it.

The next time he glanced out the window, the bathroom light glowed in the darkness of early morning. He waited for what he thought was enough time for her to shower, then went outside, stopping short of the back door.

When the bathroom light snapped off, he charged into the house, confronting Lynn in the dimly lit kitchen. "Just a minute," he said. "I need to talk to you."

"Can't it wait until I get some clothes on?"

"No, it can't wait," he said. "I've waited all night as it is." He glanced at the fluffy terry robe that wrapped her slim figure. "Besides, you're covered up. This won't take long."

She sighed and flipped on the overhead light. "All right. I'll start some coffee." She turned her back to him and pulled the coffeemaker from its corner.

He watched her movements as she poured water and measured coffee, his mind conjuring up an image of naked flesh under blue terry. Her hair was still damp from the shower, and the scent of herbal shampoo wafted his way. The urge to put his arms around her and pull her close threatened to overpower him, and he had to do something to distract himself. He jerked out a chair and sat down at one end of the little table.

"If it's so important, you might as well start talking," she said. "You don't have to wait for me to finish here."

"I want your undivided attention," he replied, realizing he really wanted to watch her reactions.

She sat in the chair at the side of the table. "Okay. What's so important?"

"You and that ghost of a husband of yours." He hesitated as her eyes opened wide, then plunged on. "Pete told me last night that you've never even looked at the evidence your brother-in-law gathered after your husband died." He watched as her face turned pale.

"What if I haven't?" she asked. "That's no business of yours." She bounded from the chair. "I'm not going to listen to this."

He was on his feet immediately and grabbed her by the arm before she could escape to the other room. "Oh, no, you don't. You're not running from me this time. You're going to hear me out."

"I don't have to listen to anything." She hissed the words through clenched teeth.

"This time you do," he said. "You say it's none of my business? Well, I've decided it is."

She tried to tug out of his grip, but he grasped the other arm and held her in front of him. "Listen to me," he said. "You made me face up to myself. You made me see that I could still throw pots of artistic quality."

"That has nothing to do with Nick," she said, glaring at him.

"Yes, it does," he replied. "You butted into my life and badgered me until I faced up to my guilt and my fears. Now I'm going to do the same for you."

"It's not the same thing," she said, trying to wriggle out of his grasp. "There's nothing you can do."

"That's where you're wrong," he replied, tightening his hold. "I'm going to badger you in return until you finally look at the evidence, finally allow yourself to believe that Nick is dead. You have to stop being afraid to live without him. Even though there's no body, you can still bury him and your guilt and get on with your life."

"You're being cruel." She snapped out the words. "Leave me alone." She tried to turn away.

"Look at me," he said. He released one arm and grasped her chin in his hand, turning her head until her blazing eyes were directed right at him.

"You have a Late Death Registration," he continued, "issued by the court. Pete says such a document is very difficult to get, that the evidence has to be more than circumstantial. The judge believed Nick died that day. So should you."

"I can't," she said, "and there's no way you can force me to. I didn't see his body."

"Lynn! You're *never* going to see it!" he shouted. "And you know that as well as I do."

"Don't yell at me."

"And I always thought I was stubborn," he said. He let go of her chin and she pulled her arm from his grasp.

"Give it up, Vince. Nothing you can say is going to convince me."

He felt like shaking her and was glad he no longer had ahold of her, or he might have followed through on the urge. Then he realized the coffeepot had stopped gurgling. "The coffee's ready," he said. "Where are your cups?"

She reached into the overhead cupboard and slammed two pottery mugs on the counter. He poured the coffee and carried both cups to the table.

When he sat down across from her, he gazed into cold blue eyes. "Do something for me," he said in as calm a voice as he could muster. "Just go look at the evidence your brother-in-law accumulated. See what's there. You're never going to finish grieving for Nick unless you do."

"I'll look at it sometime," she replied, "but I'm not ready yet. I don't even want to think about that awful day. And you keep bringing it up, again and again."

"Lynn. A year and a half is long enough to live with a ghost. Give yourself a break. Take a chance on life."

"You don't understand," she said.

"Yes, I do," he replied. "You're afraid to face reality. Just like I was. I've confronted my fears. It's your turn."

Her eyes lifted to his. "What do you mean, you've confronted your fears?"

"I finally admitted to myself that I was afraid of the future. That I was hiding behind my guilt. I'm trying to forgive myself for my part in Damon's death, realizing that he has to share the blame."

When he saw her eyes brighten he forged ahead. "I'm consciously giving up my guilt, taking a risk," he said. "I'm doing what you told me I should do. And it's working. The proof's out there in the garage."

She smiled tentatively. "What do you mean? Are you making more little squatty pitchers?"

"Better than that," he replied. "I have some new things to show you. I'm even working with different clays. Come take a look."

She glanced down at her robe. "Later, after I've had a chance to dress and eat breakfast."

"Stop on your way to the shop," he said, standing. He refilled his coffee cup. "I'll return the cup later. And you think about what I've said." He headed for the door.

As soon as the door shut behind him, Lynn set her cup down and headed for the bedroom. She dressed and returned to the kitchen for her usual breakfast of cereal and toast. She thought about what Vince had said, the part about experimenting with new forms. She forced thoughts of Nick from her mind, as she usually did, except when she was on the pier. She'd think about him later.

Pushing open the side door to the garage, she stepped into the brightly lit interior and found Vince standing by a bank of shelves, rearranging the pieces sitting on the middle shelf.

He turned at the sound of the door and a smile lit his face. "Come look. Give me your honest opinion."

Lynn stopped at his side and gazed at the eight porcelain vases displayed there. They were exquisite! Each had a different shape, a different pattern and color combination of glaze decoration, a different impact on her own artistic sensibilities. She couldn't even begin to pick out a favorite.

"You've done it!" she exclaimed. "Each one is uniquely artistic in its own way. They're magnificent."

"I won't tell you how many I ruined in the process," he said with a laugh.

She smiled up at him. "That's not important. The results are what counts."

"Now, the big question," he said. "What will you do with them?" He looked at her thoughtfully. "Do these go to that L.A. gallery?"

"I have contacts in Carmel and Monterey, too," she said. "Why don't we promote you as a local phenomenon?"

"The potter guru of Garrett Cove?" He frowned. "I'm not sure about that. I had that kind of notoriety on Long Island. Don't think I want to go through it again."

"Then I guess we send them to the Irvington in Los Angeles and see what happens."

"I'd prefer that," he replied. "I'm really a very private person. I'd like to stay here, live a simple life and work in relative isolation."

"Won't Garrett Cove be too dull for you after you become rich and famous?" she asked.

"Rich and famous!" He laughed. "You're rushing things a bit, I think." He gestured toward the vases. "This is just a beginning. I have a lot of work to do. Besides, *you're* here in Garrett Cove."

She heard the tenderness in his words and looked into the dark depths of his eyes.

"I'm sorry I got so upset with you this morning," he said.

"I realize what you're trying to do."

He dropped a soft kiss on her lips, then stepped away from her.

At the gentle touch of his lips, her heart began a staccato pounding she was sure he could hear. Just that light contact was enough to set her pulses racing. Would it be so wrong to give in to the desires smoldering inside her?

Yes, she decided. She couldn't do it. She had to get her mind back on business. "I'll call my friend at the Irvington," she said. "I'm sure she'll want the whole batch. She's very impressed with your work."

"Thanks—for all you've done for me," he said, his tone sincere.

"I'm glad to help a friend—an artist in need."

"I wish you'd let *me* help a friend," he said. "A woman who needs to learn to live in the present, instead of the past."

"Don't start on that again—please," she said.

"I have to. You've done so much for me. I have to repay the debt."

"I can't just forget Nick."

"I'm not asking you to forget him," he said. "I'm asking you to acknowledge that he's dead. Nothing more."

"I can't."

"Take off that wedding band," he said, "and put it away. That might help."

She fled from the garage.

Seven

Lynn waited two days before venturing into the garage again, hoping Vince wouldn't bring up the subject of Nick. Vince was bent over the wheel, working on what looked like a teapot. She glanced at the shelf where all the new vases had been. They were gone. Panic struck her.

"The vases—where are they?" she asked. "What did you do with them?"

He turned around and smiled when he saw her. "In those boxes over there," he said, pointing to two cardboard boxes under a table.

"You had me worried for a minute."

He quirked one brow. "Oh? I was simply waiting for you to come to me."

She detected a subtle message in the tone of his voice. "I came for the vases," she replied. "Nothing else."

"If you'll wait a minute, I'll help you carry them down to the shop."

"You don't have to," she said. "I can take two trips or use my car."

"I want to help you."

There it was again, that subtle message. His words had a double meaning she was determined not to acknowledge.

"If you insist," she said with a shrug, "but it's really not necessary."

He finished off the rim of the vessel he was shaping, then cut the pot from the wheel. "This needs to dry a bit, anyway, before I add the spout and handle," he said. "I have plenty of time to help a... friend."

Lynn watched from near the door as he placed the pot on a slab on the table, then rinsed his hands in a bucket and dried them. She hardly recognized the old towel she'd given him when he'd first moved his things into the garage. It was stained from the clay. Then she realized it was one of the towels she and Nick had received as a wedding present, the blue ones that used to be trimmed with a delicate pink satin ribbon.

There she was, thinking about Nick again. She was doing far too much of that lately. And if he wasn't on her mind, Vince was. How had her life gotten so complicated?

Vince picked up one box from under the table, handed it to her, then picked up the other and pushed open the door with his foot. "Let's go."

She glanced at him ruefully. He'd become such a big part of her life and thoughts. And she hadn't a clue what to do about it.

Later that evening, as she tried to concentrate on the novel she was reading, she heard the back door open.

It had to be Vince heading for the bathroom. Then the kitchen door opened, and her muscles tensed. She put a marker in the book and closed it.

"Lynn. Are you in there?"

At the sound of Vince's deep voice, she relaxed a bit, but not completely. It was not like him to come looking for her in the house. But certain things were changing in their relationship, subtle things. He was deliberately crossing the invisible barriers she'd erected around herself, and she couldn't seem to prevent him.

"I'm in the living room," she called, not wanting to get up from the protective corner of the couch.

When he stepped into the room and glanced around, she realized he'd never been as far as her living room before. She saw the expression on his face when he spotted the slender vase decorated with lavender iris that sat on the buffet against one wall. His smile was the gentlest one she'd yet seen.

"You kept my favorite," he said. "My grandmother used to grow iris at her cottage on Long Island."

"I couldn't sell all of them," she said. "They were too beautiful."

"I'm glad you didn't," he replied.

He stood in front of her, so tall, so masculine. It felt strange, having him in her living room. He seemed to fill the tiny room with his presence.

He frowned as if in remembrance. "At first I wanted all those pieces to be gone," he said, "so I'd never have to look at what I used to be able to do.

Then I regretted my decision. I'm glad you saved one."

She smiled. "That's what I figured would happen sooner or later. Sit down."

He lowered himself to the middle of the couch just a short distance from her.

As she gazed at him, so close, the room suddenly seemed warmer. "Was there something you wanted?" she asked nervously.

"To see you," he said with a grin as he extended one arm along the back of the couch toward her. "I was pacing the floor out there, thinking about you—" the expression on his face became serious "—and I decided to see what you were doing tonight."

The pounding of her heart heightened the tightness in her chest. "Nothing much. Just reading . . ."

All her instincts told her she should send him away. Something was different about him tonight. He didn't have that look about him that signaled a willingness to do battle. She could handle the arguments.

His hand dropped to her shoulder and began a slow sensual massage that lit a flame deep inside her. Her lips parted as she glimpsed the glow of desire in his eyes. She needed to get up from the couch. Now.

But something kept her there. His touch? The look in his eyes? Or her own needs?

He pulled her into his arms, and she went willingly, closing her eyes and savoring the feel of being so close to him.

His lips found hers and his invading tongue sent shivers of desire racing through her. The questions in her mind changed slightly. Could she send him away now? If not, could she let him make love to her? Could she make love to him?

Behind her closed lids, she tried to conjure up an image of Nick. But instead, she saw the dark depths of Vince's eyes, the rugged planes of his face, his lean powerful physique.

She wanted him. It was as simple as that. And as complicated. But she'd deal with any problems later. Now, in his arms, she felt more complete than she'd felt in... She didn't remember how long.

His lips withdrew from hers and began pillaging her neck, her throat, and his hands went on their own exploration, finding and cupping her breasts. She could no longer deny herself his touch. Her own hands caressed his shoulders, crept around his neck, then tangled in the fringe of hair at his nape.

He unbuttoned her flannel shirt and undid the front closure of her bra. She drew in a breath as his lips traveled from her throat to her breasts. When his lips brushed her nipples, she shivered and pulled him closer. His touch was light and teasing, and it was driving her wild. She arched into him.

"I want you...and not just for now...forever...." His words were almost a moan.

She wasn't sure at first what he'd said.

"I love you," he added. "I want to marry you. To have you by my side...forever."

A warning reverberated through her brain. "No...no." She pushed at his chest. "Don't say that. You can't mean it."

He sat up and his gaze was as soft as a caress. "But I do mean it," he said softly. "Every word. I want you as my wife. I love you."

Too much. Too fast. She pulled her shirt together, covering her nakedness. "You can't love me. It's all wrong. I can't love you. Nick . . ." His name came out as a gasp. She stared at Vince. "Please . . . go away."

"Dammit, Lynn," Vince said, all the warmth gone from his voice. "Don't do this to us. We'd be good together. Don't you see that?"

He pulled her to her feet and then over to the bedroom door, which was standing open. "Nick's not in there anymore. But I could be—with you. Marry me. Let me help you deal with your memories of the past."

"No!" she said, letting the panic she felt into her voice. "That's not the way I have to do it. I can't make that kind of commitment yet."

He grasped her chin and held it rigid so she had to look at him. "I can't wait any longer," he said. "Can't you see I'm at the end of my patience?"

His anger gave her new strength. She pushed his hand away and drew herself up to her full height. "I'm sorry, Vince," she said. "I'm sorry I can't be the woman you need."

"'Sorry' doesn't cut it," he replied. "And you *are* the woman I need. You just don't know it yet."

She turned on him. "You're asking too much, too soon."

"It's not too soon for me," he said. "Seeing you every day and not being able to hold you, to make love to you, is driving me crazy. I don't know how much longer I can live like this."

"You're the one who came to me," she said, "with the silly idea of using my garage."

He laughed. "Boy, did that plan backfire."

"If being here is the problem, then I guess you'll have to go," she said. "Get your own place. Get out of my garage."

"That's not going to solve anything for us," he replied.

"You wouldn't have to see me every day," she said. "You wouldn't be sharing my bathroom."

He faced her squarely. "If I move out of your garage," he said, "I'll also have to move out of town. I can't stay in Garrett Cove and watch you tear yourself apart over a ghost." He turned and stomped out of the house.

"Then go!" she shouted after him.

She collapsed on the couch, tears welling up in her eyes and spilling down her cheeks. What had she done? He wouldn't really leave, would he?

Several hours later lights flashing across the front window startled her awake. She realized she'd cried herself to sleep on the couch and hadn't even gone to bed. But the lights...

When she got up and looked out the window, she gasped. Vince had backed his van up to the door of the garage and was loading boxes into the back of it. He was leaving.

The intensity of her feeling of loss surprised her. If Vince left, she'd be alone again. But wasn't that what she'd been afraid of all along? Why she didn't want to get involved with another man? She had intended to build herself a life so independent she'd never need anyone else again. That's what she'd been telling herself, over and over, since Nick had died. That way she'd never be hurt again.

Since Nick had died? Did she believe that now? Did she want to believe he was dead?

She huddled into the corner of the couch and pulled an afghan around her, letting her mind wander back over all the things she could remember that Larry had told her, things that were in that file she'd never read. Never had the courage to read, she amended. She let the agonizing details wash over her. Again and again. Her tears fell freely for what seemed like hours.

Glancing out the window, she saw that the lights in the garage were out. And the van was still there. "Vince, I *do* want you. I want to be able to love you." She spoke the words aloud into the blackness of the night. "I do want to believe that Nick is dead. I'm trying. I really am."

She dozed off again on the couch, unwilling to go to bed. Unwilling to let the van and Vince out of her sight.

The first rays of daylight were creeping into the room when she awoke from her restless unrefreshing sleep. The van was still there. Relief flooded through her. Maybe there was still time. But would he still want her?

She hurried to the bathroom and took a quick shower, realizing that Vince hadn't been inside yet. He could still be asleep in the van and planning to leave when he woke up. The thought brought back the dark cloud that had settled over her when he'd walked out last night.

Rushing out the door, she almost ran into Vince heading for the house. She stared at his tousled hair and sleepy eyes. "Don't leave," she said. "Not yet. Can't you give me a little more time? A few more weeks maybe?"

"No, I can't do that," he replied coldly. "I've given you all the time my sanity will allow. I made a decision last night. I can't work here any longer. I'm leaving Garrett Cove."

The finality of his tone sparked something inside her. She wasn't going to grovel or beg. She bit back the words she wanted to say. She had her pride, too. Besides, maybe he was better off without her. He could support himself now. She knew that. And her ghost, as he chose to call it, was still hovering in the background, though diminished in stature.

"Where will you go?" she asked.

"Maybe back to Long Island," he replied, his eyes dark and expressionless. "I'll send you my new address so you can forward any checks."

She looked up at him and tried to keep her tone casual even though she wanted to fling herself into his arms and beg him to stay. "I'm glad things are working out for you," she said. "And I hope you'll come back some day."

"No," he said with finality. "There're one too many ghosts in Garrett Cove."

"I'm sorry you feel that way," she said. "But I can't ust change overnight."

"You've given me no sign that you're trying to hange at all," he replied. "The passion's there, but ot the love. You were ready to give me your body last ight, but that was all. I want you to love me as I love ou."

She couldn't deny his accusation. And she couldn't ay the words he wanted to hear. Something was still ot right in her own mind. Something unfinished.

"When are you leaving?" she asked.

"As soon as I'm packed and have your garage leared out for you."

"I see." She turned back to the house and he fol- owed her inside, stopping in the bathroom. She went n into the living room and sat down on the couch, lutching a pillow to her chest for comfort. She'd lost im.

The sound of the shower running tore her from her everie. It felt right having a man in the house again. he'd miss him terribly.

Wasn't that what love was all about? Wanting to be ith the person so much it hurt? That's what her hor- ble night had tried to tell her. She *did* love him.

Hurrying to the phone, she dialed her sister's num- er.

After a quick drive inland, she was sitting on the rocade couch in her sister's living room in a fashion- ble home on the outskirts of San Luis Obispo. Lynn lanced around the classically decorated room and smiled. Marrying a lawyer had given Carol all the material comforts.

But Lynn didn't envy Carol for that. She envied her for her good solid marriage, based on a foundation of love. Lynn wanted love, too. Vince's. If it wasn't too late.

Carol came in from the kitchen carrying a tray with teapot and cups. "Larry's on his way back home with the file. I'm glad you've finally come to your senses."

Lynn sniffed and tried to stem the tears that threatened. "I can't let him leave."

"I knew when I saw him in your shop that he was the man for you," Carol said. "I don't know why. Instinct, I guess. The way you looked at him."

Lynn gasped. "And just what makes you so all knowing?"

"Remember," Carol replied, "I was the one who comforted you after several broken romances—before you met Nick. I saw the signs right after Vince arrived. I knew it was only a matter of time."

Larry burst through the front door just then, dropped a thick file onto Lynn's lap and sat down beside her on the couch. "Take all the time you want. Read every word if you have to."

Lynn smiled wanly at her brother-in-law. "I don't think that's necessary. But I do want to see what facts were presented."

"Here, look at this." Larry shuffled through the pages until he came to one. He pointed to the page. "Here's Pete's deposition. He was practically standing next to Nick when he went overboard."

Lynn read the words through her tears, then dried her eyes and looked at several more of the documents, coming at last to the judge's opinion. After reading that, she turned to the copy of the Late Death Registration and read what it said. Then she closed the folder.

Nick was dead.

She knew it at last. But there was something else she had to do before she could go to Vince—if he'd still have her. If he was still in Garrett Cove.

Hugging Carol, then Larry, she rushed out the door.

She drove to the nearest florist shop and astounded the surprised clerk with her request. Thirty minutes later the clerk handed her a funeral wreath. A yellow banner across it read "Nicholas S. Frazer—Lost at Sea."

The traffic between San Luis Obispo and Garrett Cove had never seemed so heavy. Lynn inched along behind a truck for a good two-thirds of the way. When she pulled into the main street of town, she saw immediately that Vince's van was no longer in front of her garage. She drove up the hill and parked in her driveway.

A glance through the window in the side door of the garage told her Vince had finished his packing. He wouldn't be back. She had her garage back now—whether she wanted it or not.

Opening the door, she stepped inside and surveyed what was left. The shelves were still in place. The benches and table were stacked neatly on one wall. The Peg-Board hung on the wall, but now it was empty of tools. Only the lingering odor of damp clay gave any indication of Vince's former occupancy.

She closed the garage door and went into the house. All signs of Vince were gone from the bathroom—his soap, shaving kit, shampoo.

He had well and truly left.

She hadn't figured on his leaving without saying goodbye. But he had.

She walked through the quiet house and into her bedroom. Staring at the quilt-covered queen-size bed, she tugged the gold wedding band from her finger. A jewelry box sat on top of the dresser. She placed the ring in the box and snapped the lid closed. Then she glanced at her finger. It looked so bare without that ring. She rubbed the place where it had been. But she couldn't back down now. Nick was gone and she knew it.

But so was Vince, her heart wailed.

She retraced her steps through the house and back outside, stopping at the car to grab the wreath from the seat. Then she walked down the hill and out to the end of the pier.

The gray-green water lapped against the pier in a comforting soothing rhythm. The ocean had become a great solace to her. She'd miss her solitary vigils here. But Vince was right. It was time to get on with her life.

As a gentle breeze teased her loose hair, she lifted the wreath to the railing, read the inscription one last time, then flung it as far as she could out to sea.